Favourite Fables

THIS IS A PARRAGON BOOK.

© PARRAGON 1996.

PARRAGON
13-17 AVONBRIDGE TRADING ESTATE,
ATLANTIC ROAD, AVONMOUTH,
BRISTOL, BS11 9QD

PRODUCED BY THE TEMPLAR COMPANY PLC,
PIPPBROOK MILL, LONDON ROAD, DORKING, SURREY RH4 1JE

DESIGNED BY MARK KINGSLEY-MONKS

ILLUSTRATED BY: LORNA HUSSEY, JOHN JAMES, ANNABEL SPENCELEY,
CLAIRE MUMFORD, ANDREW GEESON, HELEN SMITH,
ROGER LANGTON AND HELEN COCKBURN

PRINTED IN ITALY

ISBN 0-75252-004-0 (HARDBACK)
ISBN 0-75252-067-9 (PAPERBACK)

Favourite Fables

· PARRAGON ·

CONTENTS

INTRODUCTION

Favourite Fables is a collection of classic tales which have been thoughtfully rewritten for a whole new generation of children. The thrill and excitement of adventure stories and fairytales has always captivated the imagination of children and this beautifully illustrated collection is certain to become a firm favourite with children everywhere, to return to again and again.

This volume brings together a selection of the very best tales from around the world. Here are nine of the timeless animal fables of the Greek storyteller Aesop and four of the wonderful folk tales told by the brothers Grimm. Five of Hans Andersen's famous fairytales are also included and three stories of adventure from the wonderful Persian collection known as the Arabian Nights.

AESOP'S FABLES

Illustrated by Lorna Hussey

STORIES INCLUDED IN AESOP'S FABLES:

THE TOWN MOUSE AND THE COUNTRY MOUSE

THE LION AND THE MOUSE

THE FOX AND THE CROW

THE HARE AND THE TORTOISE

THE FOX AND THE STORK

THE DONKEY IN THE LION'S SKIN

THE FOX WITHOUT A TAIL

THE WOLF AND THE ASS

THE DOG AND HIS REFLECTION

The Town Mouse and the Country Mouse

Once upon a time there were two little mice. One mouse was very grand and lived in the town but the other was quite different. He was a Country Mouse. He lived under the roots of an old oak tree in a small hole lined with straw and dry grass. He slept on a scrap of sheep's wool and wore a brown waistcoat he had made himself from an old grainsack.

"How lucky I am to live here," the Country Mouse said to himself. "I must invite my cousin to come and share my cosy home," but when the smart Town Mouse arrived, he looked about the little hole in dismay. What a shabby home! The Country Mouse laughed and led him to a table piled high with food.

"I have prepared a special meal," he said excitedly. "A cob of corn, fresh hazelnuts and rosy red rosehips."

But the Town Mouse wrinkled his nose in disgust.

"I cannot eat this food," he protested. "You must come and stay with me and discover what real food is like." So the next day the Country Mouse returned with the Town Mouse to his home in the big, busy city.

"This is what a home should be like," said the Town Mouse proudly as he led the Country Mouse from room to room. "I like soft carpets and comfortable furniture. There are no leaves or mud here."

Soon they were hungry. "Follow me," said the Town Mouse, "but there will be no rosehips or hazlenuts on the menu!" he added with a twinkle in his eye. The little Country Mouse gasped when he saw the wonderful spread laid out on the large dining table.

"This is *real* food," cried the Town Mouse. "Let us begin!" but as soon as he scampered across the floor two large dogs came bounding into the room, barking fiercely and the Country Mouse drew back in terror.

"I'm going back to my home!" he told his cousin. "You may sleep on a soft duck-down mattress under a satin quilt while I have only a scrap of wool for my bed. You may wear a red velvet coat with gold buttons while my clothes are patched and darned. You may feast on roast beef and chocolate cake while I live off the nuts and berries of the hedgerow. You can enjoy the excitement of the town if you wish but give me the plain and simple life any time!"

AND THE MORAL OF THIS STORY IS:

BETTER A POOR AND CAREFREE LIFE

THAN A RICH AND WORRIED LIFE

The Lion and the Mouse

There was once a mighty Lion. He was powerful and strong and when he roared, the earth shook, the parrots squawked and the monkeys ran chattering to the treetops.

All the animals were afraid of him and they called him the King of the Beasts. The little Mouse was especially frightened of the Lion for she knew that if one of his paws landed on top of her, she would be squashed as flat as a blade of grass. She tried her best to keep well away from the King of the Beasts.

One day, as the Lion slept in the shade of an old acacia tree, the Mouse was scuttling busily about her business, searching for small seeds to eat. Little did she know that her scurrying steps took her close by the sleeping Lion. Up his leg she scampered, all the time thinking he was nothing but a smooth termite hill. But as her feet ran tickling across his back the Lion awoke with a mighty roar. The little mouse tumbled to the ground and in a flash he had trapped her tail under one enormous paw.

"What is the meaning of this?" he rumbled and the Mouse shook with fright. "Do you not know who I am?"

The little Mouse could feel his hot breath singeing her whiskers and she nodded her head up and down rapidly.

"Yes, yes!" she gasped. "You are the King of the Beasts, the Lord of the Jungle, the mighty Lion."

"That is so," smiled the Lion approvingly. "Just so," and he tightened his grip on her tail.

"Oh, please have pity on me," the Mouse begged. "If you save my life today why, who knows, perhaps one day I shall save yours."

The Lion threw back his head and laughed and laughed. "*You* save *my* life?" he said. "A little Mouse save the King of the Beasts? That I should certainly like to see."

"Well, little Mouse," he continued. "You have made me laugh, so stop trembling and fear not, for I will not harm you."

Gently he lifted his paw from her tail and the little Mouse ran for the safety of the long grass as fast as her legs could carry her.

Now some days later big game hunters came to the grasslands and laid traps for the animals. The Lion loped along his usual path, sniffing the morning air, when all of a sudden he felt something heavy fall over him. The more he struggled the tighter he was held. He had been caught in a net! He groaned in despair for he feared his days were over. Far away the little Mouse heard his cry and she quickly ran through the grass to his side. "Now it is my turn to help you," she said and she began to nibble at the rope with her sharp teeth. Soon she had made a large hole in the net and the Lion crawled free.

"Thank you, Mouse," he said gratefully. "Now I can see that little friends can become great friends!"

AND THE MORAL OF THIS STORY IS:
ONE GOOD TURN DESERVES ANOTHER

The Fox and the Crow

There was once a fine Fox. He had a glossy red coat and a beautiful bushy tail. His pointed ears pricked up at the smallest sound and his sharp nose twitched at the faintest smell.

Early one evening as the Fox prowled under the old oak trees, his black nose began to prickle.

"What a wonderful smell!" said the Fox to himself. "It is better than rabbits. It is better than chickens. What could it be?" He bent his head to the ground and snuffled amongst the leaves and the grass. The tantalising smell was not down there. He sniffed again. "Where is this marvellous smell coming from?" he puzzled. He raised his nose high in the air and sniffed once more. Then he caught sight of something perched high above him on the branch of an oak tree.

It was a glossy black crow and she was holding something in her beak. Something yellow. Something tasty. Something very like cheese!

The Fox licked his lips. He badly wanted that piece of cheese. But how was he to reach it for he certainly could not jump high enough to catch the bird?

Then the cunning Fox had a clever idea. He looked up at the Crow and the Crow looked down at him.

"What a magnificent bird!" exclaimed the Fox. "Such glossy black feathers. Such a bright yellow beak."

The Crow stood quite still but she quivered with pleasure to hear the Fox's charming words.

"What sparkling eyes!" continued the Fox. "They glitter like two beads of jet. I cannot believe there is a bird anywhere in the world who could match this beautiful Crow." The Crow had never heard such flattery and she fluffed up her feathers and bobbed up and down on the branch, drinking in the bold Fox's honeyed words. Then the Fox spoke again and his eyes never left the large piece of cheese.

"I wonder if the Crow's voice is as splendid as her appearance," he said. "She would indeed be Queen of all the Birds if such a wondrous bird was also blessed with a glorious singing voice."

Then the vain Crow could not resist the chance to show off and opening her mouth wide, she began to caw loudly. Well, the wily Fox knew just what would happen next and he was waiting!

The cheese tumbled from the Crow's beak and fell straight into the Fox's open mouth. He chewed it slowly and lovingly and at last swallowed it with a happy sigh.

"Very tasty," he said, and he licked his lips as the Crow screeched with rage above his head.

"Well," said the Fox smugly. "So you *do* have a voice. My, but what a pity it is that you were not blessed with a brain!" and he sauntered off with his tail held high in the air.

AND THE MORAL OF THIS STORY IS:
NEVER TRUST A FLATTERER

The Hare and the Tortoise

There once lived a most bold and bumptious Hare. He loved to stroll around the warren with his nose held high in the air, and it was evident to one and all that this Hare considered himself to be the finest Hare in all the land. Now there was one thing that the Hare was proud of above all else. He had been blessed with strong back legs and that meant he could run like the wind. He never missed an opportunity to show off his running skills to his friends and no-one had ever been known to beat him. Or not until the day he met the Tortoise, who slowly crawled by as the Hare was bragging to his friends.

"Hurry up, hurry up, old Tortoise!" laughed the Hare. "If you went much slower the grass would grow over you!" The Tortoise stared at him coolly.

"You may rush about all you wish," he said, "but I get to where I want to be soon enough, thank you." He looked the Hare up and down slowly before continuing. "In fact, I reckon I could get there quicker than you, fast as you are." The Hare burst out laughing.

"Quicker than me? That I should like to see!" and so he challenged the Tortoise to a race.

The arrangements were soon made and the very next day everyone turned out to watch the Hare and the Tortoise run their race.

"Five, four, three, two, one, go!" cried the Fox, who was acting as umpire, and in a flash the Hare was out of sight and over the hill. The crowd clapped and cheered as the old Tortoise lifted first one foot and then the other and slowly began to make his way along the path. He looked neither right nor left but kept his eyes on the winding road straight ahead.

The Hare raced along the road and as he flashed by a great cheer went up from the people lining the course. It was obvious to one and all that the Hare was in a great hurry, but he still found time to turn and wave triumphantly to his supporters as he ran by. Far behind him the Tortoise plodded steadily on his way.

Soon the Hare had reached the race's halfway point.

"I have plenty of time," he said to himself. "I must be miles ahead of that old slowcoach by now. In fact, I could have a snooze right here and now and when I wake up, continue on my way and I would still have time to beat that Tortoise hollow!" So saying, he sat himself down and closed his eyes.

The hours passed by and after a time the Tortoise appeared over the brow of the hill. He ambled down the road until he reached the spot where the Hare sat fast asleep. The Tortoise raised his eyebrows but said not a word and continued steadily on his way. The sun was sinking in the sky when the Hare suddenly awoke. He yawned and stretched and saw to his satisfaction that the Tortoise was nowhere to be seen. "Plenty of time to win the race!" said the Hare to himself happily.

Off down the road he sped but as he came over the brow of the hill he saw the most amazing sight. There ahead of him was the Tortoise taking his last few steps towards the finish line! The crowds cheered wildly as his shiny shell broke the tape in two and the Fox declared him the winner. As the Hare panted for breath at the end of the race, the Tortoise smiled placidly. "Slow I may be but I keep my eye on the goal and I don't let anything distract me!"

AND THE MORAL OF THIS STORY IS:
SLOW AND STEADY WINS THE RACE

The Fox and the Stork

One day a Fox decided to invite a Stork to tea. He made all the preparations in the kitchen and set the table with his best crockery. He brushed his fine long tail until it shone like copper and then dressed in his best blue coat.

Soon there was a tap, tap, tap upon the door. It was the Stork and with a great flourish, the Fox opened the door and bowed low.

"Do step inside," he cried. "Welcome to my humble home." The Stork looked very elegant in a beautiful purple hat and matching cape and as she stepped daintily into the room her hat feathers quivered. She was very hungry. "I do hope the Fox has plenty of food," she said to herself anxiously.

"I have cooked some beautiful soup," announced the Fox. "Let us begin," and he showed the Stork to a chair. But the poor Stork was dismayed to see that the only plates laid upon the table were quite flat. How would she be able to eat off such a dish?

The Fox came bustling in from the kitchen and carefully set a steaming pot of soup down in the centre of the table.

The Fox ladled out the soup with much smacking of lips and many appreciative sniffs. Then he sat down, lifted his spoon and smiled broadly at the Stork.

"Do tuck in!" he urged. "This is my best soup!"

But the Stork looked down at her plate and sighed unhappily. She could not swallow this soup with her long pointed beak and so she could only sit and watch as the Fox greedily lapped up his plateful.

When the Fox had quite finished he looked across at the Stork in surprise.

"Did you not enjoy the soup?" he asked, wrinkling his brow as if greatly concerned. But the poor Stork was too polite to complain and so the wily Fox lapped up her portion as well.

The next day when the Stork awoke she was still hungry. She decided to repay the Fox's hospitality and invited him to dinner that evening. He was delighted and accepted eagerly.

But as the Fox sat down to eat at the Stork's table he could hardly believe his eyes. The only dishes upon the table were two tall jugs! The Stork dipped her slender beak inside the jug and drank her soup but the Fox could only lick his lips hungrily and watch, for there was no way he could get at the food.

He returned home a sadder and wiser Fox with nobody to blame but himself for, as he plainly realised, he had only been paid back for his own uncaring behaviour.

AND THE MORAL OF THIS STORY IS:
DO AS YOU WOULD BE DONE BY

The Donkey in the Lion's Skin

There was once an unhappy Donkey. He lived in the jungle with all the other animals but they were cruel and often made fun of him. How he wished he could get his own back on the unfriendly creatures but whenever they saw him they just laughed and called him rude names.

One day the Donkey had quite a fright. As he trotted along the jungle path he thought he saw a Lion waiting to pounce on him. But the Lion didn't move and then the Donkey realised that it was not a real Lion after all, but just a Lion's skin.

"This would make a fine costume for me to wear," said the Donkey and he slipped it over his back. He looked exactly like a real Lion!

"Now I can teach those animals a lesson," said the Donkey, and he hid in a thicket and waited for someone to pass by. Soon the Monkey came swinging along, clinging to the vines with his tail. Out jumped the Donkey with a fierce roar and the Monkey ran screeching up a tree. Then the Bear came ambling along the path but when he saw the Lion he ran whimpering into the bushes.

Then the fierce Tiger came prowling by but when the Donkey jumped out at him, he ran off into the jungle as fast as he could. The happy Donkey had never had so much fun in all his life! He stamped his hooves with glee and rocked with silent laughter.

The sun was slowly sinking in the west as the crafty Fox slunk into view. With his head bent low, he sniffed for food amongst the shrubs and grasses. He could smell all sorts of interesting things, but he could not smell danger so imagine his surprise when out rushed the Donkey in the Lion's skin! To the Donkey's great delight the terrified Fox yelped and ran for cover with his tail between his legs.

But this time the silly Donkey could not help himself and he laughed out loud. His loud bray echoed through the jungle and the wily Fox stood stock still. Slowly he walked back to the fierce Lion skin and looked under the great head. There he came face to face with the embarrassed Donkey and the silly animal hung his head low.

The Fox laughed long and loud and then all the other animals came running.

The astonished creatures gathered around the blushing Donkey and soon the jungle rang to the sounds of their catcalls and hoots of glee.

"Why, it wasn't a fierce Lion who pounced out on me after all!" cried the Monkey. "It was just the silly old Donkey," grumbled the Bear.

The Donkey looked very ashamed.

"You foolish Donkey!" said the Fox. "If only you had kept your moth shut, your trick might well have succeeded but you just had to give your game away with your loud bray!"

AND THE MORAL OF THIS STORY IS:

A FOOL MAY DECEIVE OTHERS WITH HIS APPEARANCE BUT HIS WORDS WILL SOON REVEAL HIM

The Fox without a Tail

There was once a fine Fox, a most handsome fellow with a shiny red coat and a long bushy tail. This Fox was a rather vain creature and he spent long hours brushing his tail from top to tip until it shone like bright copper.

But one evening he had a most dreadful accident. As he hunted amongst the thickets and hedgerows for a tasty meal he suddenly heard a loud *clack!* and felt the most dreadful pain.

He realised at once that he had been caught in a trap and, pull as he might, his beautiful tail was stuck fast. Suddenly the pain stopped and to his great dismay the Fox found his tail lying in all its glory upon the ground. The trap had pulled it clean off. This was a calamity! Why, he was a Fox! The best and finest Fox that ever was — and what was a Fox without his tail? Why, little more than a laughing stock! How the other Foxes would taunt him when they saw him creeping by, tail-less. The very thought of it was more than he could bear.

After a while he stood up, collected his hat and made his way to the forest dell where the Foxes met for their nightly meetings. As the Fox strutted into the centre of the circle a hushed silence fell on the entire company. He wore his best hat and tucked inside the hatband was his own fine red tail!

A young Fox began to titter, then another, then another and soon the forest rang to the sounds of their rude laughter. With a dignified expression, the Fox held up his hand for silence and spoke.

"As you know, I have been blessed with a particularly fine specimen of a tail and I have been proud to carry it around behind me ever since I was born. But now I feel the time has come for a change. Tails should not drag behind us in the dirt. No, they should be worn on high, where their beauty can be fully admired."

The Fox paraded around the glade.

"This is the new fashion" he said "so you had all better start wearing your tails on your hats, like me."

Then an old Fox stood creakily to his feet.

"We have heard what you have to say, Brother Fox, but answer me this," he said. "Would you be quite so keen for us to follow this new fashion if your own tail had not been pulled off in a trap?" Then the poor Fox saw that everyone had seen through his cunning plan and he slunk off into the forest, much ashamed.

AND THE MORAL OF THIS STORY IS:

IF YOU SUFFER SOME MISFORTUNE, MAKE THE BEST OF

WHAT YOU HAVE AND DO NOT TRY TO

MAKE OTHERS SUFFER ALSO

The Wolf and the Ass

One day the Ass set off to find some sweet grass to eat. He followed the path from the jungle and soon found himself far away from his usual haunts. Here the grass was lush and green and soon the Ass was busy chewing away, quite contented and without a care in the world.

But as he munched happily in the meadow a big grey Wolf crept up on him unawares. Suddenly the Ass pricked up his ears for he could hear the pad of soft paws behind him.

"That Wolf means to make me his supper!" said the Donkey to himself.

When the Wolf was close enough to pounce, the Ass lifted his head and called out quite calmly.

"I shouldn't do that if I was you," he said. The Wolf was astonished. Why was the Ass so unafraid?

"I have trodden on a sharp thorn," explained the Ass, "and if you eat me it will be sure to stick in your throat. I am sure you wouldn't want that."

The Wolf shook his head and the Ass continued.

"I will lift up my hoof and then you can pull out the thorn before you eat me," he offered helpfully. The Wolf could not believe his luck. He stood behind the Ass and as the Ass waited patiently with his hoof in the air, the Wolf had a good look for the thorn. But there was no thorn to be found!

Then the Ass summoned up all his strength and with a loud and triumphant whinny he gave a mighty kick. The Wolf flew head over heels into the air and landed in the middle of a thorn bush, howling with pain.

"That Ass is not as stupid as he looks," thought the Wolf to himself as he picked the thorns from his bottom, one by one, but the Ass just smiled at him sweetly as he trotted off home.

AND THE MORAL OF THIS STORY IS:
BEWARE OF UNEXPECTED FAVOURS

The Dog and his Reflection

There was once a naughty Dog. He loved to sit outside the Butcher's shop and admire the strings of shiny sausages and rows of pink pork chops. How he wished he could help himself to something to eat!

One day when the Butcher's back was turned, the Dog ran into the shop and seized a large ham bone in his strong teeth. Off down the street he ran while the Butcher waved his sharpest knife and shouted after him angrily.

"Nobody has a bone as big and as tasty as mine!" the Dog said to himself as he set off for home. But as he crossed the bridge what should he see but another Dog with another bone — and this bone was just as big as his own! The Dog was astonished.

"I shall have that bone," he decided. "Two bones are better than one!" With that, the silly Dog opened his mouth and snapped greedily.

But what a shock he got when his own bone tumbled from his mouth and landed with a splash in the water. To the Dog's great dismay the bone sank quickly out of sight and he realised he was left with

nothing at all. Slowly he trudged back to his kennel, feeling very sorry for himself. He lay down and rested his head upon his paws. What a tragedy it was to have something in your grasp and then have it snatched suddenly away.

"I was wrong," sighed the Dog unhappily. "One bone is much, much better than none."

AND THE MORAL OF THIS STORY IS:
BE GRATEFUL FOR WHAT YOU HAVE

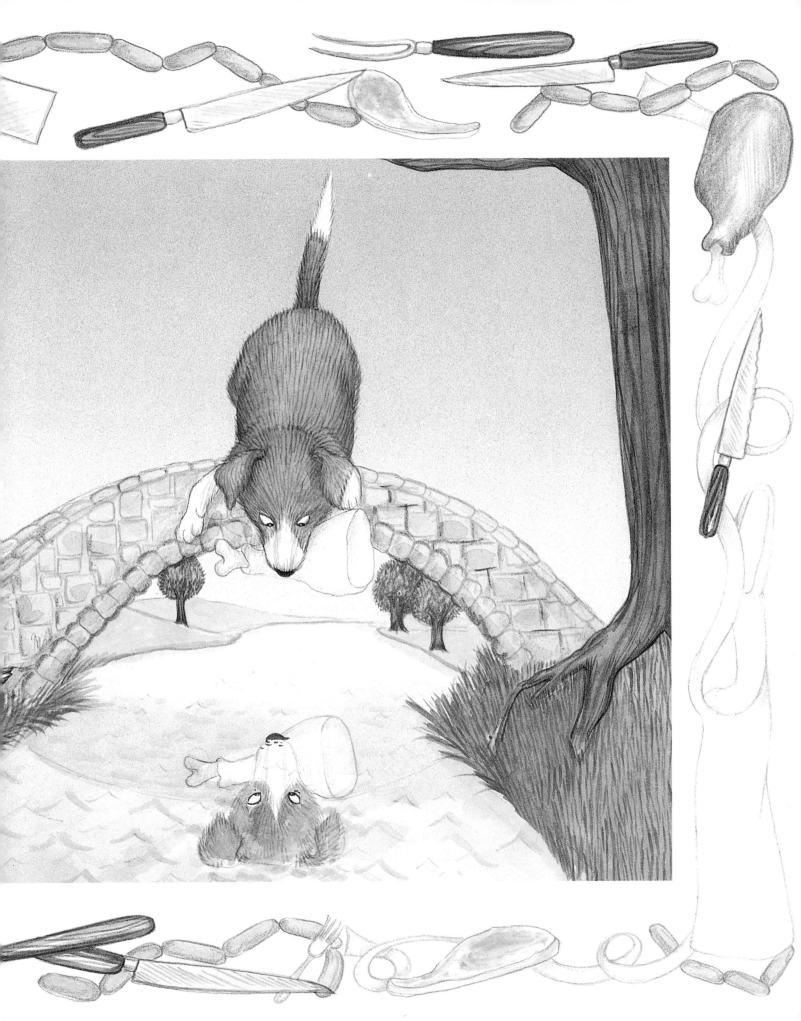

GRIMM'S FAIRYTALES

Illustrated by John James,
Annabel Spenceley and Claire Mumford

STORIES INCLUDED IN
GRIMM'S FAIRYTALES:

THE FROG PRINCE
✤
HANSEL AND GRETTEL
✤
RAPUNZEL
✤
THE GOLDEN GOOSE

The Frog Prince

Illustrated by John James

Once upon a time there lived a King and Queen. They had three beautiful daughters but the youngest Princess was so lovely that she gladdened the heart of everyone who saw her. She was a merry child and her favourite toy was a golden ball which sparkled in the sunshine.

One summer's day the sun shone from a cloudless blue sky and there was not a breath of wind to stir the air. It was so hot that the little Princess decided to play in the shade of the wood. Slowly she walked amongst the tall trees and their long shadows were cool and soothing after the glaring heat of the sun.

Soon she could hear the sound of splashing water and, following the sound, she came upon an open glade where a fountain tumbled into a silvery pool. What a lovely sight! With a cry of delight, the Princess threw her ball high into the air and ran to catch it — but to her dismay the ball slipped through her fingers, rolled over the ground and fell into the pool.

With a cry of alarm she knelt by the pool and tried to reach it but the ball quickly sank from sight. How she wept at the loss of her precious toy.

Her tears fell into the pool and ripples spread over the still, grey water. Suddenly she heard a little voice.

"Princess, why do you weep so sadly?" it said, and to her surprise, there sat a green frog on a large lily pad.

The Princess sighed deeply. "I have lost my golden ball," she explained, wiping a tear from her cheek. "I fear it is gone forever." The Frog spoke again.

"If I find your ball for you, you must promise me something in return," he said solemnly.

"I will promise you anything!" cried the Princess.

"You must promise me that I can eat from your own golden plate and sleep in your own golden bed, and then I will fetch your golden ball," said the Frog.

The Princess did not like the sound of this at all!

"I will pretend to agree to what he says," she decided, "but as soon as I have my ball I will run home and he will never be able to find me." And so that is just what she did and the poor Frog was left alone on his lily pad.

That evening as the Princess sat down to eat she had forgotten all about the Frog in the pond. But the Frog had not forgotten her. He had found his way to the palace and at that moment was sitting outside the door.

Suddenly the Princess heard a small voice.

"Open the door, my Princess dear.
Open the door to your true love here!
And remember the words that you and I said
By the fountain cool in the greenwood shade."

"Who is that, my daughter?" asked her father, the
King. Then the unhappy Princess explained all that had
happened in the wood and her father looked grave.

"You must honour your promise," he said. "The Frog
kept his word and now you must keep yours."

The Princess opened the door with a heavy heart and there sat the Frog. Slowly she returned to her seat and the Frog followed, *flip, flop, flip, flop.* The Queen, the Princess's two elder sisters and all the Ladies-in-Waiting shuddered with horror as the warty little creature passed by, and when he hopped upon the table they moaned and hid their faces in their napkins.

The Princess wrinkled her beautiful nose in disgust as the Frog crept close to her plate and with a long darting tongue ate up her peas one by one. At last he sat back and yawned.

"Now I am sleepy," he said. "Please take me to your room for I wish to sleep upon your pillow."

The Princess was horrified. She looked imploringly at her father but the King shook his head.

"It may seem hard, little daughter," he said, "but you must do as he asks. A promise is a promise." So she carried the Frog upstairs and soon he lay fast asleep upon her silken pillow. The Princess vowed she would not sleep a wink all night but after a while her eyelids drooped and soon she, too, slept. The next morning when she awoke the Frog was nowhere to be seen.

"At last I am rid of the horrid creature," thought the Princess to herself— but she spoke too soon! That evening as she sat down to eat her meal the same little voice could be heard outside the door.

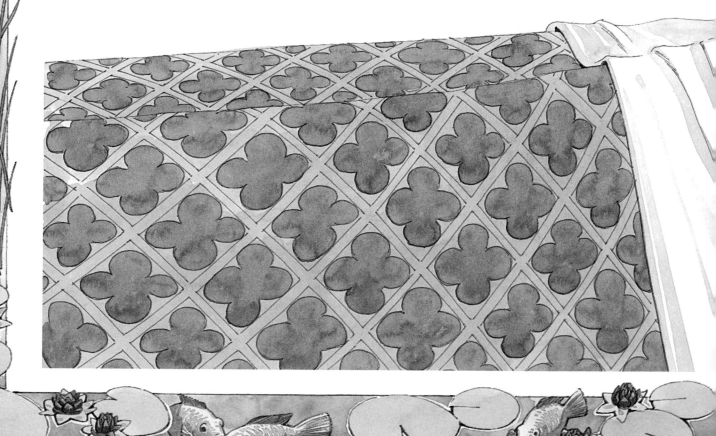

"Open the door, my Princess dear.
Open the door to your true love here!
And remember the words that you and I said
By the fountain cool in the greenwood shade."
There sat the Frog once again, and once again he asked to eat from her plate and once again the Princess had to do as he wished. There he sat upon the linen tablecloth and the Ladies-in Waiting shrieked in disgust as the little creature happily licked the cherries on top of the iced cakes.

When he had eaten his fill he asked to be taken to the Princess's golden bed and there he slept as before upon her silken pillow. The little Princess had no choice but to sleep by his side and after much shedding of tears she fell fast asleep beside him.

The next morning the sunbeams crept through her bedroom window and as they touched her soft cheek, the Princess awoke. She opened her eyes slowly, dreading the sight of the Frog beside her on her pillow. But he was nowhere in sight.

Instead she found herself gazing into the eyes of the most handsome Prince she had ever seen.

"Sweet Princess, please accept my deepest thanks," he said as he took her hand. "You have saved me from a wicked spell. An evil witch turned me into a Frog and banished me forever to the fountain pool. The only person who could break the spell was a Princess who would let me eat from her plate and sleep on her pillow." The Prince stroked her hair gently.

"You did this for me, ugly as I was, and now the spell is broken and I am free." He knelt upon one knee.

"Please marry me and share my happiness forever," he begged. The Princess agreed at once and so they were married and when the wedding was over a white coach pulled by eight white horses pulled up outside the palace. It was driven by Faithful Henry, the Prince's servant, and as the happy man jingled the reins, the joyful couple drove off to begin their new life together.

Hansel and Grettel
Illustrated by Annabel Spenceley

Once upon a time long ago there lived a poor woodcutter and his two children, Hansel and Grettel. The children's mother had died when they were very young and their father had married again. Their stepmother was a wicked woman and she did not love Hansel and Grettel. The woodcutter had very little money to spend on food and so all four of them went hungry for much of the week.

Late one night as the two children lay shivering in their beds they heard their stepmother talking.

"Something must be done or we will all starve to death," the woman whispered to the children's father. "We have enough food for two mouths, but not for four. We must get rid of Hansel and Grettel."

Grettel wept bitterly as she heard her stepmother describe how she would lead the children deep into the forest and leave them there to perish.

"I will find a way home, little sister," said Hansel.

The next morning the children were taken far away.

"Stay here until we return," said their stepmother. Soon night fell and they were left quite alone.

Poor Grettel sobbed as if her heart would break.

"Dry your eyes, little sister," said Hansel. "On the way here I dropped a white pebble on the ground every few steps. See how they shine in the moonlight. We can follow the trail home." Sure enough, the pebbles showed them the way perfectly and some hours later they were pushing open the door of their house.

Their father was overjoyed to see them for he had bitterly regretted agreeing to his wife's plan. Their stepmother pretended she was pleased but they could clearly see the disappointment on her face.

Some days later Hansel and Grettel heard her talking to their father once more.

"We are hungrier than ever," she complained. "We must try and lose the children again tomorrow." This time Hansel did not have time to collect a pocketful of white pebbles so when they were led into the forest he dropped a trail of crumbled bread for them to follow that night. But when they searched for the crumbs they were dismayed to find them all gone, for the birds had eaten every one!

"We are lost!" cried Grettel.

Again and again they tried to find a way out of the forest but every path they took led them ever deeper into the wood. Suddenly Hansel saw a white dove sitting upon a branch. She twittered at them, then flew off over the trees.

"I believe she is telling us to follow her," said Hansel and with weary steps they trudged after the little bird. She sang as if to encourage them on their way and after a time they found themselves in an open glade. And there in the middle of the clearing was the most perfect little gingerbread cottage.

"Oh, Hansel!" gasped Grettel. "The roof is made of honey cake and the windows are made of barley sugar! I must just nibble a little corner." Soon they were both munching away on their favourite bits of the house and nothing had ever tasted quite so delicious.

All of a sudden the door flew open and out hobbled an old dame leaning upon a stick. The children drew back in fear but the old lady smiled at them kindly.

"Welcome to my home, my dears," she said. "Come inside and I will look after you." She fed them sweet pancakes, then put them to bed under cosy quilts.

But when Hansel and Grettel awoke next day the old lady's kind manner had changed. Her weak eyes glinted cruelly as she grabbed Hansel by the arm.

"You will make a tasty morsel for me to eat," she cackled and then the children saw that they had been tricked. The old lady was a witch and she meant to make a meal of them! Laughing cruelly, she bundled Hansel into a cage.

"I will fatten you up before I cook you," she hissed and Hansel shook with fear. Every day she checked to see how fat he was getting but clever Hansel stuck an old bone through the bars and when the old crone pinched it, she decided he was still too thin to eat.

At last the witch could wait no longer.

"Fat or thin, I will eat him as he is," she decided, clutching at Grettel with one claw-like hand. "And you will help me prepare the cooking pot."

How the little girl sobbed as she carried the water and lit the fire under the oven. The witch scowled at her and stamped her feet.

"Stop your wailing," she shouted. "Just climb in the oven and tell me how hot it is." Then Grettel had a clever idea. She looked up at the Witch timidly.

"I don't know how to climb inside the oven," she said anxiously. "Can you show me?"

The witch stamped her foot again, but moved close to the oven entrance.

"Why, you silly goose," she said crossly, "it is perfectly simple. All you have to do is put one foot here and then you can step right inside." But as the witch showed her where to put her feet Grettel suddenly ran at her and with a great shove pushed the old hag right inside the oven and slammed the iron door tight shut. Gracious, how the old witch yelled! Soon Hansel was free from the cage and jumping for joy.

Then the two children explored every inch of the gingerbread cottage, upstairs and down and hidden in every corner were chests full of treasure. Jewels and pearls, gold and silver — the children could hardly believe their eyes! They filled their pockets to the brim and little Grettel held as much as she could hold in her apron.

Soon they were ready and they set off to find their way home. After a while they came to a large lake but they could find no way of crossing the water.

"Now we will never see Father again," sighed Hansel, but just then a large white duck came swimming by.

"I will carry you over on my back," she offered and so the two grateful children were delivered safe to the other side. For many hours they walked under the shade of the trees and after a time the forest began to look more familiar and then, to their delight, Hansel and Grettel saw their own little home in front of them.

Their father wept for joy as he gathered the children into his arms for he had not had a single happy hour since he had lost them.

"Your wicked stepmother has gone away for good," he said. "Now we will be together forever."

The Golden Goose
Illustrated by Claire Mumford

Once upon a time there were three brothers. The youngest son was given the name of Dummling and was laughed at by his family and everyone else.

One day the eldest son went into the forest to cut some wood. His mother gave him cake and a bottle of wine and off he went, whistling cheerfully. But he had no sooner set to work than a little old man appeared.

"I am so hungry and thirsty. May I have some cake and wine?" he asked. But the eldest son shook his head.

"Be off with you," he said gruffly. "I will share my meal with no-one." But it seemed the old man was going to get his revenge with the very next swing of the axe for it landed on the eldest son's foot. How he yelled! The next day the second son decided to try his luck and once again his mother gave him cake and wine.

The little old man approached the second son and asked to share his meal, but the second son also refused. He, too, was cut by the next swing of the axe.

The next day Dummling set off for the forest to cut some wood. He was given only bread and water but was happy to share what he had with the little man.

"You are a good boy," said the man, "and if you cut down that tree you will get your reward." Dummling did as he was bid and was astonished to find a goose covered entirely with golden feathers.

"I will go to the city and seek my fortune," Dummling decided. "This beautiful goose will bring me luck." As he strolled along the lane he passed a girl. She gasped to see such a glorious golden bird and stretched out her hand to stroke it. But imagine her dismay when she found that she could not take her hand away! The goose had magic powers and whoever laid a finger on her soon found themselves stuck fast to her feathers.

Before many hours had passed Dummling had collected two more inquisitive girls and a Parson, all stuck fast one behind the other. As they stumbled across the fields they met the Bishop.

"My dear Parson!" he cried. "Have you taken leave of your senses?" and he reached out and caught the Parson's sleeve. Now he, too, was stuck fast and it wasn't long before they were joined by a ploughman and a shepherd!

After a time they reached the city and there in the palace lived the King and his daughter. She had never been known to smile and the King had promised her hand in marriage to the first person who was able to make her laugh. Well, when the Princess saw the three girls, the Parson, the Bishop, the ploughman and the poor shepherd all falling over one another behind Dummling's golden Goose, she burst into peals of laughter.

The King came running and Dummling lost no time in asking permission to marry the Princess.

"Hmm," thought the King to himself. "I do not want this raggle taggle boy to marry my daughter. I must set him an impossible task to perform and when he fails, I will be able to refuse him."

And so the King told Dummling that before the marriage could take place he would first have to find a man who could drink a whole cellarful of wine.

Dummling scratched his head and then he remembered the old man in the forest. But when he returned to the glade the old man was not there. Instead, he found a short man with a miserable face.

"Oh, my, I am so terribly thirsty," he moaned. "I have already drunk a barrel of wine but I feel as if I could drain a lake dry!"

"You are just the man I am looking for!" cried Dummling and he led the man to the King's cellar.

The fat man rubbed his hands with glee.

"This is a sight for sore eyes!" the short man declared and soon he had emptied every bottle, keg, cask and barrel. The King was more vexed than ever. He decided to set another task and this time made it even harder.

"Find me a man who can eat a whole mountain of bread," he ordered, well satisfied that this would indeed prove impossible.

But Dummling went straight to the forest and there discovered a tall, thin man sitting on a log.

"I have just had four ovenfuls of bread for my supper but it has barely taken the edge of my appetite," he complained. Dummling pulled at his sleeve.

"I know a place where you can eat your fill," he said.

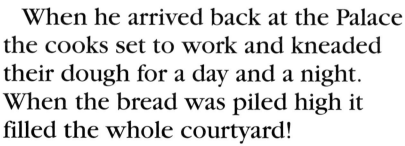

When he arrived back at the Palace the cooks set to work and kneaded their dough for a day and a night. When the bread was piled high it filled the whole courtyard!

The tall, thin man ate and ate and ate and within hours the mountain had become a molehill, and soon there was nothing left at all.

Then the King set one last impossible quest.

"Find me a ship which can sail both on land and on sea. Only then can you marry my daughter," he declared.

This time Dummling found the little old man waiting for him in the forest.

"I have not forgotten your kindness," he said. "Now look behind you." Then, with a great rustling of canvas, the most magnificent ship sailed into the glade.

When the King saw the ship sailing over the fields towards his palace he knew he would have to give in and so Dummling and the Princess were married.

They lived happily ever after but back at home Dummling's two brothers grew bitter and miserable — and all for the lack of a good, generous heart.

Rapunzel

Illustrated by Annabel Spenceley

There once lived a man and his wife. They were good, simple people but they were not happy for they longed for a child. At last the woman grew so sad that she fell ill and took to her bed. From her window she could see into the garden of the big house that stood next door. This house belonged to a witch and the garden was surrounded by a high wall so everyone kept well away. But the more the woman gazed into that garden, the more she longed to taste the fresh, green herb that grew there.

"You must fetch me some of that rampion herb to eat or I shall surely die!" she said at last to her husband. So one night when all was dark the man climbed the wall and hastily gathered a handful of leaves. Soon he was back home, safe and sound and as his wife tucked into the herb she began to feel much better.

But as the days passed she fell ill a second time and begged her husband to fetch her more of the health-giving herb. So it was that he climbed the wall again. But this time the witch was waiting!

"How dare you creep into my garden and steal my rampion like a common thief?" she demanded.

The poor man fell to his knees, covered his eyes and quivered like a leaf.

"Forgive me!" he begged. "My wife could see the plant from her window and it looked so good that she longed to taste it." This compliment softened the witch a little, but then her eyes grew cunning.

"I shall let you go free on one condition," she hissed. "Your wife will soon have a baby but when it is a week old you must give it to me." The man was so terrified that he would have agreed to anything.

"Yes, yes," he gasped and without a backward look he scrambled over the wall and ran for home.

Some months after this, his wife did indeed have a baby daughter and great was their joy. But on the seventh day after her birth the witch swept into the room, plucked the child from the cradle and was gone! The man and his wife were grief-stricken but however hard they searched, they never saw the witch or their daughter again.

The witch raised the little girl all alone and named her Rapunzel, for that is another name for the rampion plant. When Rapunzel was sixteen the witch locked her away in a tall tower in the middle of the forest and each day she would visit her and call out:

"Rapunzel, Rapunzel, let down your golden hair!"

Then Rapunzel would let her long plaits fall from the window and the witch would hold on and climb up hand over hand.

So the time passed and poor lonely Rapunzel would sing to herself to while away the hours. Her voice was like sweet birdsong and one day it was heard by a Prince who was riding by. He hid behind a tree when the witch arrived and watched as she clambered up into the tower. He longed to meet the girl with the lovely voice and so when the witch had gone, he climbed up Rapunzel's plaits and jumped inside the room.

Rapunzel was astonished to see this handsome stranger kneeling before her but he spoke to her gently.

"Have no fear," he said. "You have won my heart with your beautiful singing and now my happiness would be complete if you would agree to become my bride."

Rapunzel did not need to think twice and soon they they had planned her escape.

"I will bring you a length of silk thread each day and you must make a secret rope-ladder," the Prince decided and then, with a shy kiss, he climbed down Rapunzel's long plaits and rode away. So she worked night and day on her ladder and hid it carefully under the bed when she heard the witch calling.

But one day she made a big mistake. As the old crone pulled herself up the side of the tower Rapunzel leaned out of the window and watched her.

"Why does it take you so long to climb up?" she asked. "The Prince climbs up in no time at all." Then the witch seized her by the arm and shrieked with rage.

"I thought I had hidden you safe from all the world and now you have managed to deceive me. You will suffer for this, you wicked girl!" She grasped a sharp pair of scissors in one hand and, snip, snap! soon Rapunzel's beautiful golden tresses lay upon the floor. Then she took the frightened girl far off to a bleak and lonely place and left her there all alone.

That evening the witch lay in wait for the Prince. Soon she could hear his strong voice ringing out,

"Rapunzel, Rapunzel, let down your golden hair!"

The witch tied Rapunzel's plaits to a hook on the wall and threw them out of the window. In a trice the Prince had scrambled up and leapt inside, but what a shock he got to find not his beloved Rapunzel but the horrible witch awaiting him!

"Ha, ha, ha!" she cackled. "Your little bird has flown! I have hidden Rapunzel far, far away and you will never see her pretty face again."

The Prince was filled with despair and the sight of the evil witch so revolted him that he jumped right out of the window. He landed in the rose bushes that grew around the foot of the tower and their sharp thorns pierced his eyes. He was blinded and, hardly knowing what he was doing, he wandered off through the forest in search of his sweet love.

The birds and beasts brought him food to eat and without their nuts and berries he would surely have starved to death. The animals listened sorrowfully as he wept for the loss of his lovely bride but they did not know where she was hidden and they could not help.

So the Prince strayed through the wilderness for many weeks and with each step his heart grew heavier and heavier.

The little birds tried to lift his low spirits by singing to him, but their song could not compare to that wonderful voice he had heard so long ago in the tall tower. The months passed by until one day a new birdsong was carried to him on the faint breeze and his heart stopped still.

He had heard that song once before. Could it be his Rapunzel? He stumbled blindly towards the sound and although he could not see her, Rapunzel looked up and saw her Prince at once. She ran into his arms and held him close. As she wept for joy two of her tears dropped on his eyes and suddenly they grew clear and he could see as well as ever.

"You will never be parted from me again," he promised Rapunzel, and so they made their way to his kingdom and there they were married. They heard no more from the wicked witch and Rapunzel and her Prince lived happily ever after.

HANS ANDERSEN'S FAIRYTALES

Illustrated by Andrew Geeson, Helen Smith,
Roger Langton and Annabel Spenceley

STORIES INCLUDED IN
HANS ANDERSEN'S
FAIRYTALES:

THE UGLY DUCKLING
✀
THE STEADFAST TIN SOLDIER
✀
THE LITTLE MERMAID
✀
THE LITTLE MATCHGIRL
✀
THE SWINEHERD

The Ugly Duckling

Illustrated by Andrew Geeson

There was once a little mother duck. She had six eggs in her nest and there she sat day after day in the summer sun patiently waiting for them to hatch. Five of the eggs were small and white but the sixth egg was large and brown. The little duck often wondered why that egg was so different.

One morning she heard a crack, then another, then another. Her chicks were ready! One by one they tumbled from their shells and soon five little chicks were gathered under the wings of their proud mother. But the large brown egg had not hatched.

"What can be keeping my last little chick?" thought the mother duck to herself and she settled herself on top of the egg to keep it warm.

At last she felt the egg moving and out scrambled a chick. But this chick was nothing like her other babies. He was covered in dull brown fluff and had a long scrawny neck. He wasn't nearly as pretty as his brothers and sisters. But the mother duck loved him just the same and took care to protect him from the other farmyard animals who often teased him.

"Did you ever see anything quite as ugly as that gawky looking creature?" squawked a large brown duck to his friend, the white hen.

"Go away!" clucked the hen. "We don't want you in our farmyard," and she pecked at the poor little duckling with her sharp beak.

Not a day passed by without one animal or another making fun of the duckling so at last he decided he would run away. One dark night he crept away quietly while everyone was asleep and headed for the open fields. By daybreak he was quite exhausted.

"I will rest for a while," he said to himself and was soon fast asleep. But he awoke just two minutes later to feel the hot breath of a large animal wafting over him. Peeking out from under his wing he was terrified to see a fierce beast with a long red tongue! It was a hunting dog but to the duckling's great relief it simply sniffed him and then padded away across the moor.

"I am too ugly even for that dog to eat!" thought the duckling to himself sadly and he waddled off in search of somewhere to live. Not far away there was a cottage and for a time the duckling stayed there with an old lady, her hen and her cat. But they were not like him and as the days passed he longed to find some water so that he could splash about and swim.

"I must find a pond," he told the cat as he waved them goodbye. The weather grew colder and the snow began to fall. Suddenly the duckling heard a strange sound high above him and looking into the sky he saw a flock of white geese flying south for the winter.

The duckling watched them go, spellbound. He had never seen anything so beautiful in all his life.

"If only I could go with them!" he sighed, "but what would those lovely creatures want with an ugly companion like me."

On he trudged and at last he reached a little pond — but how wretched he was when he saw that the water had turned to ice! There was one small patch of freezing water and there he splashed for a while but the cold had sapped his strength. Soon he found he could not get out of the water and back onto the land. After a while the ice crept closer and closer and then he was trapped. The duckling would surely have died if a man had not happened to pass by at that very moment. He saw the little creature stuck fast in the ice and took him home and warmed him in front of the fire. So the duckling spent the next few weeks being cared for by the kind man and his wife.

Soon the weather grew warmer and the duckling longed to be on his way once again.

"I must find a proper home for myself," he explained to the man and his wife as he waddled away.

The air grew softer, the birds sang and the flowers bloomed in the meadows once again. The duckling felt stronger and he noticed that his feet and his body had grown much bigger and seemed to be changing colour. He felt happy and excited and, stretching out his wings, he beat them up and down for fun. Just imagine his astonishment when he suddenly found himself leaving the ground and flying through the air! What a glorious feeling it was to be soaring on high.

"Here in the sky I am free!" he said to himself happily. All at once he saw something exciting far below him. As he swooped down to get a better look he recognised the snow white birds who had flown over him on their way south. Now they had returned and were splashing in the pond. The duckling landed on the water and slowly swam towards them.

"I know I am ugly," he said shyly, "but please let me stay with you and be your friend."

"Why, you are not ugly!" laughed the birds. "You have become a beautiful swan just like us," and as the duckling bowed his head to look in the water he saw that it was indeed true!

The Steadfast Tin Soldier
Illustrated by Helen Smith

There was once a Tin Soldier. He was exactly the same as his twenty-four brothers, but for one thing. He had only one leg! When he was made, the tin ran out just as it was about to be poured into his second leg, but he could still stand straight and tall.

He lived in the nursery with all the other toys but his favourite by far was a pretty little lady who stood on one toe and pointed her other foot high in the air. Why, it was almost as if she had only one leg, just like him! She was made all of paper and held her arms gracefully above her head, for she was a Dancer.

The Steadfast Tin Soldier loved to watch her and stood perfectly still for hour after hour gazing at her lovely face and wishing he could speak to her.

"But what is the use of trying to win her love?" he sighed. "She lives in a grand castle and I have to share a wooden box with my twenty-four brothers."

The toys belonged to a little boy and soon it was his bedtime. Gradually the house grew dark and still. Everyone was asleep. Now it was time for the toys to have their fun!

Out of their boxes and bags they jumped and soon the nursery was full of spinning tops, bouncing balls and dancing dolls. But there were two toys who did not move at all. They were the Tin Soldier and the pretty Dancer. They stayed quiet and still, each standing on their one leg as they gazed silently at each other.

Suddenly the grandfather clock chimed midnight and with a loud *snap*! out from the snuff box jumped a little black imp.

"Why do you keep staring at the Dancer?" he asked the Tin Soldier. "Do you not know that it is considered very rude to stare?" But the Tin Soldier did not reply. He did not even look at the Imp but continued to gaze at the lovely paper lady.

The Imp stamped his foot angrily. "Why, of all the impertinent creatures!" he snorted. "First you stare and now you ignore me. You just wait. You will learn your lesson tomorrow!"

The next day the little boy played with the one-legged Tin Soldier and when he went for his tea he left him standing on the windowsill. Now whether it was the wind or whether it was the little black imp up to his tricks, who can say, but all of a sudden the window flew open and the Soldier was blown outside!

Down he tumbled and with a bump landed upside down between two paving stones. There he stayed, firmly wedged, while the little boy searched high and low. If only the soldier had called out he would have been found in an instant but he was proud and felt that no soldier should have to call for help. The little boy returned indoors and soon it began to rain. The raindrops fell faster and faster and before long there was a real downpour.

When the rain stopped two little street urchins came by and they soon spotted the Tin Soldier.

"Let's make a paper boat!" cried one, "and then we can sail him up and down the gutter like a proper Sea Admiral." Soon the Tin Soldier was standing stiffly to attention in his own newspaper boat while the water rushed him along the gutter.

All of a sudden the boat entered a dark tunnel and the boys' excited shouts were left far behind.

"Oh, dear!" said the Tin Soldier to himself. "This is all the fault of that little imp. If only I had the Dancer sitting alongside me I should not care one jot but it is rather frightening on my own." But he did not show his fear for an instant. He stood straight and tall with his gun held stiffly on his shoulder.

Suddenly a great water rat poked his head out of the water beside the boat and the Tin Soldier thought his end had come. But the boat sped on by and then the Tin Soldier saw a circle of light ahead of him. With a great rushing of water, the paper boat was swept into daylight and over a great waterfall, for this was where the gutter emptied into the canal.

The water hissed and boiled around the little boat and the flimsy paper could take no more. It slowly fell apart and the Tin Soldier sank below the surface, still standing proudly to attention. As the water slid over his head all he could think of was the peaceful face of the little Dancer.

Suddenly the Tin Soldier heard a loud *gulp*! and to his great surprise found himself in total darkness. He had been swallowed by a fish! After a short while the fish began to twist this way and that and just when the Tin Soldier felt he could bear it no longer, all was still once again. There he lay shouldering his gun and wondering what on earth was to become of him.

The hours passed and just when the Tin Soldier truly believed he was lost forever there came a blinding flash of light and he found himself lying on a table.

The Tin Soldier had had quite a journey. The fish had been caught on a hook and taken to market. There it had been bought and was now lying silver-bright on a kitchen table, ready to be cooked.

"Why, it's a little Tin Soldier," exclaimed the cook.

"I will take him upstairs to the nursery."

So it was that the little Tin Soldier found himself standing on a table and looking into the face of a little boy. Well, what strange things do happen in this world! He was in his old nursery and there was the pretty Dancer still standing on one toe the same as she always did.

But the boy was not pleased to see the Tin Soldier. Maybe it was because he looked so shabby, or maybe the little black imp had something to do with it, but he snatched up the Tin Soldier and threw him in the fire!

There he stood, as brave as could be, and the flames flickered around him. He looked straight at the paper lady and she looked right back at him.

Suddenly the door opened and a draught picked the paper lady off the table and carried her through the air. Straight towards the fire she floated and there she landed right in the arms of the Tin Soldier. As her arms brushed his cheek she burst into flames and was gone. Then the Tin Soldier finally melted.

The next morning when the maid swept out the fire she found a cinder of black paper and a small lump of tin in the shape of a heart — all that was left of the Dancer and her Steadfast Tin Soldier.

The Little Mermaid

Illustrated by Roger Langton

Far, far out to sea, where the water was deep and blue, the Mer People swam in their underwater grottoes. The Mer King had a fine palace made all of coral and there he lived with his six daughters. They loved their life under the sea but when the youngest daughter caught her first glimpse of the upper world, she thought it was the most wonderful place she had ever seen.

One evening the little Mermaid watched spellbound as a fine ship came sailing close by. She was near enough to see a young man in one of the cabins. He was a Prince and the Mermaid thought him the most handsome man in the world. Suddenly there was a loud clap of thunder and black clouds rolled across the sky. The wind whipped the waves as high as hills and, to the Mermaid's great terror, the great ship was struck by lightning and split right in two. The sea was full of men, all shrieking and wailing and there, clinging to a spar, was the handsome Prince. She took hold of his arm and, swimming strongly, towed him to land.

As he lay upon the beach a young girl found him and called for help. The Prince opened his eyes and believed that she was the one who had saved him. Only the little Mermaid, hiding behind a rock, knew the real truth. Before the Prince could ask who she was, the young girl ran off and so the Prince's rescue remained a mystery. But the little Mermaid could not forget him and every evening she swam to the surface of the sea and gazed at the palace where he lived.

"Come home with us," said her sisters, but the Mermaid longed to catch another glimpse of the Prince.

"You cannot share his life," they scolded. "You have a silver tail and will never be able to walk on dry land. You must forget him." But the Mermaid could think of nothing else. She would not be happy until she was rid of her tail and able to visit the upper world.

Far away, in a cave made from the bleached bones of shipwrecked sailors, there lived the Sea Witch.

"Perhaps she will be able to help me," said the little Mermaid to herself. "She frightens me dreadfully but I can think of no other way to win my heart's desire."

Through forests of slimy seaweed and across wild, frothing whirlpools the Mermaid swam until she reached the Witch's lair. The Witch listened to the little Mermaid's request as snails crept across her lap and a large green frog squatted upon her shoulder.

"I can take away your tail and give you those two stalks that men call legs," said the Witch at last, "but you will have to give me something in return. I want your sweet voice so I warn you, from the moment you drink my potion you will be struck dumb!" The Mermaid could think only of her Prince and agreed to this terrible demand at once.

"When you walk on land," added the Witch, "every step will be as if you are treading on sharp knives. Are you sure you want to endure this pain?" The Mermaid nodded quickly as she thought of her dear Prince and their life together in the upper world. Quickly she drank the magic potion and in a trice her tail turned into legs.

She found herself lying upon the marble steps beside the Prince's palace and when she was discovered by the Queen's maids she was dressed and brought before the royal family. They were all captivated by her beauty and sweet nature but when they asked who she was, the Mermaid could not say a word.

Gentle music filled the air and the Mermaid could not help but dance. She moved gracefully across the floor, spinning and twirling, but every step was agony and soon her eyes were filled with tears. The Prince held her in his arms and felt great pity and tenderness for the little girl but it was clear to the Mermaid that he did not share the same love that she had for him. As the weeks passed the Prince showed nothing but kindness to the Mermaid, but she longed for a love to equal her own.

Soon the time came for the Prince to take a bride and the King and Queen announced that he would marry the daughter of a neighbouring king. As the Prince was introduced to the Princess the little Mermaid thought her heart would break for the girl was the same girl who had knelt by the Prince's side on the beach so long ago.

"You are the one who saved me!" cried the Prince, but the silent Mermaid could not explain the truth.

That night, as the happy couple slept aboard the royal ship, the little Mermaid looked sadly out to sea. All at once she saw her sisters rise up from the deep.

"Take this knife," they called. "The Sea Witch says that if you kill the Prince and let his blood fall upon your feet you will once again become a Mermaid!"

But as the Mermaid gazed upon his innocent face she knew she could never harm him and she threw the knife far overboard. Then, with one last look at her love, she jumped over the rail and into the foaming sea. She could feel herself melting away as she slowly became like the sea froth dancing above the crashing waves. Then, as a thousand sweet voices filled the air with song, she felt herself raised up high.

"Join us, little Mermaid," sang the voices. "We are the spirits of the air. We do not need the love of man for we can live forever." As she rose into the air, the Mermaid could see the Prince and his bride sleeping peacefully far below her and she was glad that they had found true happiness together. Then the Mermaid turned away, stretched out her gossamer arms, lifted her face to the sun and everlasting joy filled her heart.

The Little Matchgirl
Illustrated by Annabel Spenceley

It was New Year's Eve and the little matchgirl clutched her bundle of matches in a hand that was numb with cold. All day long she sat huddled on the pavement but not a single person stopped to buy and she had not earned so much as a single penny. She was very hungry but knew she could not return to her poor home until every match had been sold. She shivered as the icy wind whipped around her bare feet and the snow fell in flurries about her head.

Everyone was hurrying back to their houses to celebrate the start of a new year. The delicious smell of roast goose wafted on the air and the sound of happy laughter could be heard from across the street.

The little matchgirl looked at the matches in her lap. Maybe if she lit just one it would give her some warmth, if only for a little while.

With trembling hands she struck a match against the wall and how it spluttered and blazed! She curled her hand around the match to protect it from the wind and as the girl gazed into the flame she thought she could see something wonderful.

There was a big stove glowing with a splendid fire! But just as she stretched out her feet to warm them, the match went out and the stove was gone.

How desperate the little girl felt when she looked at the burnt-out match in her hand. She simply *had* to feel that comforting warmth again. Slowly she took another match and struck it once more upon the wall. It blazed up and where the light fell upon the bricks they became transparent and the little matchgirl was sure she could see right through and into the room on the other side.

There was a table all laid for dinner and in the middle sat a large roast goose, glistening and golden. The matchgirl could smell the savoury meat and her eyes shone as she looked at it hungrily. It seemed to come closer and closer—then the light went out and there was nothing to be seen but a cold black wall.

"Just one more match!" said the little girl to herself and this time the flame showed her a beautiful green Christmas tree covered with glowing candles. But in no time at all the match had burnt down and the tree disappeared. But the candles had not gone. Their bright little lights rose higher and higher until the matchgirl could see that they were twinkling stars.

Suddenly one of them fell across the sky.

"Someone is dying," thought the little girl. "My dear grandmother used to tell me that when a star falls, a soul is going up to God." She struck another match against the wall and this time she gave a cry of surprise for there was her grandmother in a warm circle of flame and she looked so very happy.

"Grandmother!" cried the little girl. "Oh, do take me with you. You will vanish when the match goes out, just like the warm stove, the delicious goose and the beautiful tree. Please do not leave me here!"

Then the little matchgirl struck match after match against the wall because she wanted so much to keep her grandmother near her. The light of the matches made the night as bright as day and grandmother had never looked so beautiful. Gently she gathered the little girl in her arms and together they soared in a halo of light and joy far above the earth where there was no more cold, no hunger and no pain, for now they were with God.

And as the cold morning light crept over the horizon it found the little girl huddled against the wall. She was dead but her pale face shone with a wonderful smile.

The Swineherd
Illustrated by Annabel Spenceley

There was once a Prince who decided he would find himself a bride. He had his heart set on marrying the Emperor's daughter and so he sent two special gifts to win her love. In one casket was a rose blossom with a scent that was sweet enough to make you forget all your cares and sorrows and in the other casket perched a little nightingale with a song that would make your heart sing.

But when the Emperor's daughter saw these treasures she stamped her foot and sent them away.

"What do I want with a silly flower and a brown bird?" she pouted. "I prefer jewels and toys." But the Prince would not give up so easily and, dressed as a peasant, he went to the Emperor and asked for work.

"The only job I have is for a Swineherd," replied the Emperor. "You will find your lodgings with them." And so the Prince was made Imperial Swineherd and given a horrid little room next to the pigsties in which to live.

He worked busily all day and soon he had made a beautiful little cooking pot.

If you held your finger in the steam you could smell what everyone in the palace was cooking for their dinner, from the Lord Chancellor's roast beef right down to the scullery maid's thin gruel.

The next day the Princess came by and when she heard the magical, musical pot she sent her lady-in-waiting to ask what it would cost. What a shock!

"The Swineherd is asking for ten kisses from Your Royal Highness!" the maid gasped. The Princess was outraged by this impertinence but the more she thought of the pot, the more she wanted it and so at last she gave in and the Swineherd took his ten kisses.

The magic pot was a great success but the Swineherd did not stop there. He set to and made a singing rattle and when he swung it around his head it played the jolliest of waltzes and polkas. When the Princess heard the rattle she was determined to make it hers. But how dismayed she was to hear that this time the naughty Swineherd wanted a hundred kisses!

"It is a terrible thing for the Emperor's daughter to be seen kissing a Swineherd," said the Princess, "but I must encourage a true artist and so I will do as he asks."

From his window the Emperor could see a little crowd clustered in front of the pigsties.

"What are the ladies-in-waiting up to now?" he said. "I will tiptoe up behind them and find out." Softly, softly he crept into the pig yard and there he saw his beloved daughter in the arms of the filthy swineherd!

"What is the meaning of this?" he thundered as he fell about the Swineherd with his slipper. "You are both banished from the palace!" and the poor Princess and the disguised Prince were locked outside the gates.

"Now what is to become of me?" wailed the forlorn Princess. "If only I had married that Prince while I had the chance." Then the Swineherd went behind a tree and changed out of his dirty clothes. When he next stepped before her he was dressed as a fine Prince and the Princess blushed and curtsied prettily in front of him.

But the Prince was not impressed. "You did not appreciate my gifts of the rose and the nightingale," he said sternly, "but you would kiss the Swineherd for a silly musical pot! You have made your bed and now you must lie in it!"

And so the Prince returned to his own kingdom and left the Princess with only a pot and a rattle for company.

TALES FROM THE ARABIAN NIGHTS

Illustrated by Helen Cockburn

STORIES INCLUDED IN
TALES FROM THE
ARABIAN NIGHTS:

ALI BABA AND THE FORTY THIEVES
⚬
ALADDIN AND THE MAGIC LAMP
⚬
SINBAD THE SAILOR

Ali Baba and the Forty Thieves

Far away in the land of Persia there lived two brothers, Ali Baba and Cassim. Ali Baba was a poor man but Cassim was wealthy and lived in a fine house with plenty to eat and drink. Sadly, his wife was a greedy woman and always wanted more.

Ali Baba was chopping firewood in the forest one day when he heard the sound of horse's hooves. He feared that robbers might be coming so scrambled up a tree to safety. Silently he watched as a large body of men rode past and pulled up by a sheer rock face. The leader of the men dismounted and strode up to the rock.

"Open, Sesame!" he cried, and to Ali Baba's great amazement a secret door swung open. Ali Baba counted as the men slipped inside the opening and disappeared from view.

"Forty robbers!" he said to himself. "I wonder what they have hidden inside that cave." Some time later the robbers emerged and galloped away. Then Ali Baba slid down from the tree and stood by the rock face.

"Open, Sesame!" he cried, and lo and behold, the rock door slid open and he quickly ran inside.

Ali Baba expected to find a dark and dismal hole but to his great astonishment the cave was full of the most magnificent treasures. Fine silks lay in bundles upon the floor and exquisite jewels were scattered round about. Great coffers and chests overflowed with gold coins and yet more gold was heaped up in piles around the walls. Ali Baba rubbed his hands with glee! Now he need never go hungry again. Quickly he gathered up as much gold as he could carry and hurried home.

Ali Baba's wife was overjoyed to see the money.

"Please let me weigh it before you hide it away," she begged her husband and she borrowed a set of scales from Cassim and his wife, her nearest neighbours.

"I wonder what she wants them for?" puzzled Cassim's wife. But when the scales were returned to her later she discovered the truth because in her haste, Ali Baba's wife had left one gold piece in the bottom of the pan. Cassim's wife was jealous.

"Ali Baba has so much money he does not bother to *count* it," she told her husband. "He simply *weighs* it!" Then Cassim lost no time in asking Ali Baba where he had found so much gold. Honest Ali Baba explained what he had seen and offered to share the treasure with his brother. But the wily Cassim decided he would go to the cave alone and take all the treasure for himself. Early the next day he set off with his donkeys.

"Open, Sesame!" he cried and, sure enough, the cave door swung open. Hurriedly he filled sack after sack with jewels and gold coins but when he wished to leave he could not remember the magic word to open the door and let him out again!

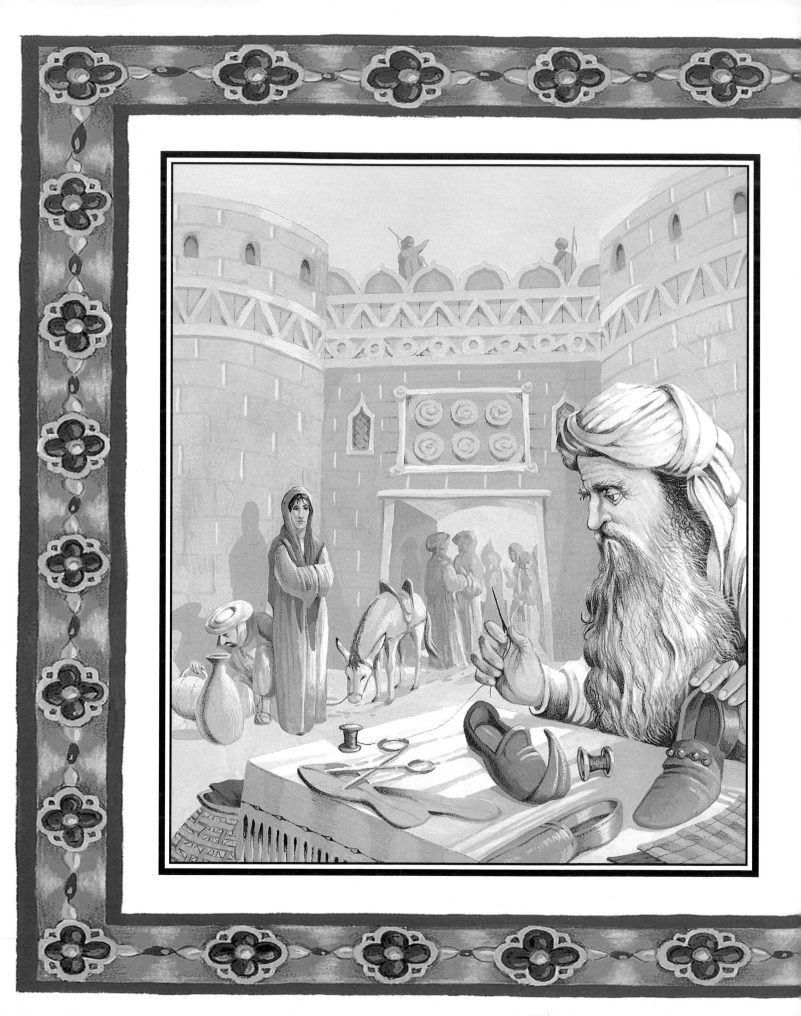

Cassim tried name after name but the door stayed firmly shut. After a while, to his great horror, he heard the trampling of horse's hooves outside the cave. In rushed the robbers and they fell upon him with their long sabres and cut him into four quarters. Then they left him there as a lesson to any other intruder.

That night Ali Baba went in search of Cassim and what a dreadful sight awaited him when he entered the cave. Sadly, he carried home the four quarters of his body and laid them on the table. Cassim's wife wailed and sobbed but Ali Baba's servant, a clever woman called Morgiana, remained calm.

"I will find a cobbler to stitch the four quarters together," she decided, "and then the body can be buried peacefully." So saying, she set off for the market and there she found an old cobbler hard at work.

"I have a job for you, old man," she whispered, "but you must not breathe a word of it to anyone." Then she tied a blindfold around his head and led him to the house of Ali Baba. The cobbler stitched away at the four quarters and late that night Morgiana blindfolded him once more and led him back to his stall.

When the Forty Thieves returned to their cave they were astonished to find that the body was missing.

"Someone else knows our secret password!" cried the Captain. "He must be found!" One of the robbers was sent to the city to discover all he could and as he entered the city gate the first person he saw was the old cobbler. When the robber offered him a gold coin, the cobbler told him all that had happened.

"I am sure I could find the house again," he said and soon he had led the robber to the very door.

The cunning robber marked the door with a cross and returned to his Captain, well pleased. But when Morgiana returned from market she saw the mark and guessed what had happened. Quickly she chalked crosses on all the other doors along the street, so that when the robbers returned that night they were confused and unable to trace the exact house.

The next day the Captain himself went to see the old cobbler and asked once again to be shown the house where he had stitched the body. This time the Captain stared hard at its windows and doors. He would not forget this house in a hurry! Then he went to the market, bought forty mules and forty oil jars, and returned to his cave. One jar was filled with oil and then each robber climbed inside an empty jar and, after the jars were lashed to the mules' backs, they set off for the city.

Disguised as an oil merchant, the Captain stopped outside Ali Baba's house and knocked on the door.

"I am taking my oil to sell at the market tomorrow," he said, "but now I need somewhere to stay the night. Can you help me?" Kind Ali Baba invited him inside and sent the mules to be stabled in the yard.

Later that night the Captain crept into the yard and whispered his orders to his men, still hiding in the jars.

"Be ready to fight when I give you the word!" he hissed, then tiptoed back inside to join his host. Ali Baba had invited him to join them for a meal and Morgiana was busy cooking in the kitchen.

"I was not expecting visitors," she fussed to herself, "and now I have run out of oil!" Then she remembered the oil jars in the yard. "I am sure the merchant will not mind if a take a little for my cooking," she said to herself as she hurried outside with her jar and lamp. Suddenly she heard a voice — and she was sure it came from inside one of the oil jars!

"Is it time to fight yet, master?" it said. Then Morgiana knew that these were the robbers come to attack her master and, filling her lamp with oil, she quickly ran back inside the house. She boiled a large pan of oil and when it was scalding hot she tipped it over each of the robbers until they were all dead.

At midnight the Captain tried to rouse his robbers but without success. When he discovered each one had been killed he fled over the wall and was gone.

The next morning Morgiana told Ali Baba of all that had happened and he thanked the clever girl for saving his life. But back in the lonely cave, the Robber Captain sat hatching a different plot to kill him.

This time he disguised himself as a rich cloth merchant and set up a stall opposite Ali Baba's house. As the days passed the unsuspecting Ali Baba grew quite friendly with the merchant and invited him to dine at his house.

But as soon as the merchant arrived at the door clever Morgiana knew who it was straight away.

"Fetch your drum!" she told Abdallah, the kitchen servant. "I will dance for my master and his honoured guest." Ali Baba, his son and the pretend merchant lay upon silk cushions on the floor. As the drum beat grew louder, Morgiana whirled around the room, each time coming ever closer to the wicked Robber Captain.

Suddenly Morgiana whipped a small dagger from her belt and plunged it into the Captain's chest.

"You wretched girl!" cried Ali Baba. "What have you done?" Quickly Morgiana explained that the cloth merchant was none other than the Robber Captain.

"See here!" she cried, and she pulled a knife from his sash. "He meant to kill you with this!" Then Ali Baba praised her courage and as a reward for her loyal service he gave her permission to marry his son, for the two had long been in love.

And so Ali Baba's family lived happily ever after and in time he told his son the secret of the cave. As his son grew older he, too, passed on the magic password to his children and so the years passed in prosperity and great contentment for them all.

Aladdin and the Magic Lamp

Once upon a time there lived a lazy boy called Aladdin. His father was dead and his poor mother despaired of her good-for-nothing son ever finding himself a job for he spent all his time running around the street markets and teasing the stallholders. One day a stranger approached him. "Are you Aladdin?" he asked, and the boy nodded.

"I am your father's brother and have been away for a long time," explained the man. "Now I am back and would like to give you work." When Aladdin's mother heard this news she was overjoyed and welcomed the stranger to their home. But what the trusting woman did not know was that this was no uncle but a scheming magician who was looking for a boy to help him.

"I will buy you some new clothes," said the pretend uncle to Aladdin, "and then you must come with me on a short journey." The next day they walked for many miles into the country and soon the town was left far behind. The boy's feet ached and he longed to go back.

"We are here," said the magician at last and he made a small fire. Throwing on some strange powders, he chanted a magic spell and the earth trembled under their feet. To Aladdin's astonishment a stone slab appeared in the ground. The magician pulled it back to reveal a flight of steps leading down and out of sight.

"You are to follow the steps into a secret garden and there you will find a lamp," said the magician. "Bring it to me and I will reward you well." Then he gave the boy a ring. "Wear this for protection," he said.

The Garden was full of beautiful trees sparkling with the strangest fruit Aladdin had ever seen.

"I will take some home with me," he said, then he found the lamp and returned to the top of the steps.

"Hand me the lamp and you can come out," ordered the magician and his eyes glittered cruelly. Aladdin shivered. He did not trust this man.

"First give me my reward," he insisted. The magician had not expected this and he flew into a rage.

"Do you not know who I am, you foolish boy?" he cried and he slammed the stone slab shut. Then the angry magician fled far away to Africa, leaving poor Aladdin trapped in the dark cave. For two whole days the boy wept bitterly then at last he fell to his knees and prayed for help. His fingers rubbed the ring and suddenly a huge genie appeared in front of him.

"What is your wish?" thundered the genie. "I am the Slave of the Ring and will obey you in all things."

Aladdin lost no time in wishing to be taken home and soon found himself back with his mother.

"Why would the wicked man want this dirty old lamp?" she wondered and she gave it a rub.

With a huge flash, another enormous genie appeared and bowed low before them.

"I am the Genie of the Lamp!" he cried. "Your wish is my command!" Quickly Aladdin ordered food and drink and soon he and his mother were eating off silver dishes. Then Aladdin showed his mother the strange fruit that he had picked.

"This is no fruit, my son," she gasped. "These are the biggest jewels I have ever seen. We are rich, rich!"

"And look at these fine silver plates, mother," said Aladdin. "We can sell these and need never worry about money again." So they hid the jewels and sold the plates and lived happily for many months.

Now the ruler of this country was a mighty Sultan and he had a lovely daughter. On certain days she would go to bathe in the springs of a lovely garden close by Aladdin's home. It was forbidden to look at the Princess as she passed by but Aladdin was filled with a desire to see her face. One day he hid behind the gate and caught a glimpse of her as she passed by.

The Princess was so beautiful that Aladdin fell in love with her there and then. He had to win her heart!

"The Princess would never marry you!" laughed his mother. "She will want to marry a rich Prince." But Aladdin begged her to visit the palace and ask the Sultan's permission.

"You can give him our jewels as a gift," he added.

When the Sultan saw the jewels his eyes lit up.

"Any man who owns such riches as these must be deserving of my daughter's hand," he said. But his chief minister, the Grand Vizier, was most displeased for he wanted the Princess to marry his own son.

"You must set the young man a difficult task to fulfil," he advised. "He must prove that he is worthy of the Princess." Then the Sultan rubbed his chin thoughtfully.

"Tell your son he must bring me forty basins of gold, overflowing with jewels, and they must be carried by forty strong slaves," he said at last. When Aladdin heard this he rubbed the magic lamp and the genie burst forth from the spout and bowed low. The very instant that Aladdin made his request, his house became full of jostling slaves, each carrying a bowl of fine jewels.

Aladdin's mother led the way to the palace and when the Sultan saw the procession he was lost for words.

"This must be a very wealthy man indeed," he thought to himself and he happily gave permission for Aladdin to marry his daughter. At once the happy boy began his preparations. With another quick polish of the lamp he summoned the genie.

"I need a set of clothes fit for a Prince," he said, "and then you can build me a palace for us to live in." The new palace was magnificent. The walls were gold and silver and the windows were surrounded by diamonds.

Soon Aladdin and the Princess were man and wife.

But far away in Africa the magician had not forgotten the magic lamp and after several years had passed he returned to the city to seek it out. The first thing he saw was the grand new palace twinkling in the sun.

"That is where Prince Aladdin and his bride live," an old man told him. "The Prince is the richest man for miles around." The magician ground his teeth in rage for he knew that the lamp had won him this wealth.

One day Aladdin left on a hunting trip and while he was away the magician thought of a plan. He disguised himself as a peddler and arrived at the palace gate with a basket full of shiny new copper lamps.

"I will swap my new lamps for your old lamps!" he cried, and the Princess heard him from her window.

"What a strange idea!" she laughed. "Take him this dirty old lamp if he wants it," and, not knowing its value, she handed her maid the magic lamp.

"Would you take this old lamp?" the maid asked the magician and the wicked man nearly shouted for joy. Quickly he grabbed the lamp and sped from the city. As night fell he rubbed the spout and roused the genie.

"Take the Princess and her palace back to Africa with me," he ordered, and in a flash it was done. The next day the Sultan was horrified to find that the palace and his beloved daughter had disappeared.

"Aladdin has tricked you!" cried the Grand Vizier. Then the enraged Sultan ordered that Aladdin be captured and put to death. When the townspeople heard the news they were angry and shouted out for Aladdin's release. The Sultan hesitated for the Prince was very popular. At last he decided to show mercy.

"I swear to you that I will find the Princess," the boy promised when he was found. "If I should fail then you can punish me however you like."

So Aladdin's life was spared and he left the city to seek his wife. But it was as if she had disappeared into thin air. No-one knew where she was and no-one could help him. Many days passed by and at last he threw himself on his knees and prayed. As he did so, he rubbed the magic ring he still wore on his finger. With a flash of light the genie appeared before him.

"Take me to the Princess," begged the delighted Aladdin and in a trice he found himself outside her window. Soon she was in his arms and telling him all that had happened. Then Aladdin understood. The Genie of the Lamp had a new master. Carefully he handed the Princess a small packet of powder.

"Pour this poison into the magician's wine," he said, "and all our troubles will be over." They could hear the wicked man approaching so Aladdin quickly hid.

"Do have a glass of wine," urged the Princess to the magician, then she waited until his back was turned and tipped the powder into his glass. Sure enough, with the very next sip of his wine, the magician fell lifeless to the floor. Then Aladdin burst from his hiding place and found the lamp inside the magician's coat.

"Your true master has returned," he told the Genie. "Now take us back home!" And so Aladdin lived happily ever after and wherever he went he always took great care to keep his magic lamp well hidden!

To his amazement he found the ground was covered with glittering diamonds. Just then Sinbad heard a hiss and spinning around he saw six large serpents slithering across the rocks towards him. He turned and ran and at last found a hiding place in a hole in the ground. There he hid all that day and all through the night and at last the serpents gave up and crawled away.

Suddenly a a huge lump of meat fell on the ground in front of him. Then another, and another. With a loud flapping of wings a great eagle landed on one large piece of meat and took off into the air again. Sinbad remembered a story he had heard about the men who lived in these parts. They had devised a special way of gathering diamonds. They threw meat down into the valley and the jewels would stick to the soft flesh. Then the eagles would grab the meat and fly with it to their nests. There the hunters picked the diamonds from the meat and so both eagles and men were happy! Quickly Sinbad tied himself to a piece of meat. This could be his way out of the valley! Sure enough, an eagle took the meat and flew off to his nest. What a shock the hunter got to see a man landing there!

From the mountain top Sinbad found his way to the coast and set sail once again but this time his ship was blown off course by a violent wind. They came close to an island and saw to their horror that the sea was full of strange monkey-like creatures swimming towards them. Soon they were crawling on the decks and swarming up the rigging.

The Ape Men took over the ship and forced Sinbad and his shipmates to jump overboard and swim for land. They set off to explore the island and soon found a deserted palace. In the courtyard was a huge mound of what looked suspiciously like human bones but the men were so tired that they decided to rest there for the night. Suddenly a loud roar filled the air and in through the gate strode the most horrible one-eyed ogre. The sailors sat rooted to the spot.

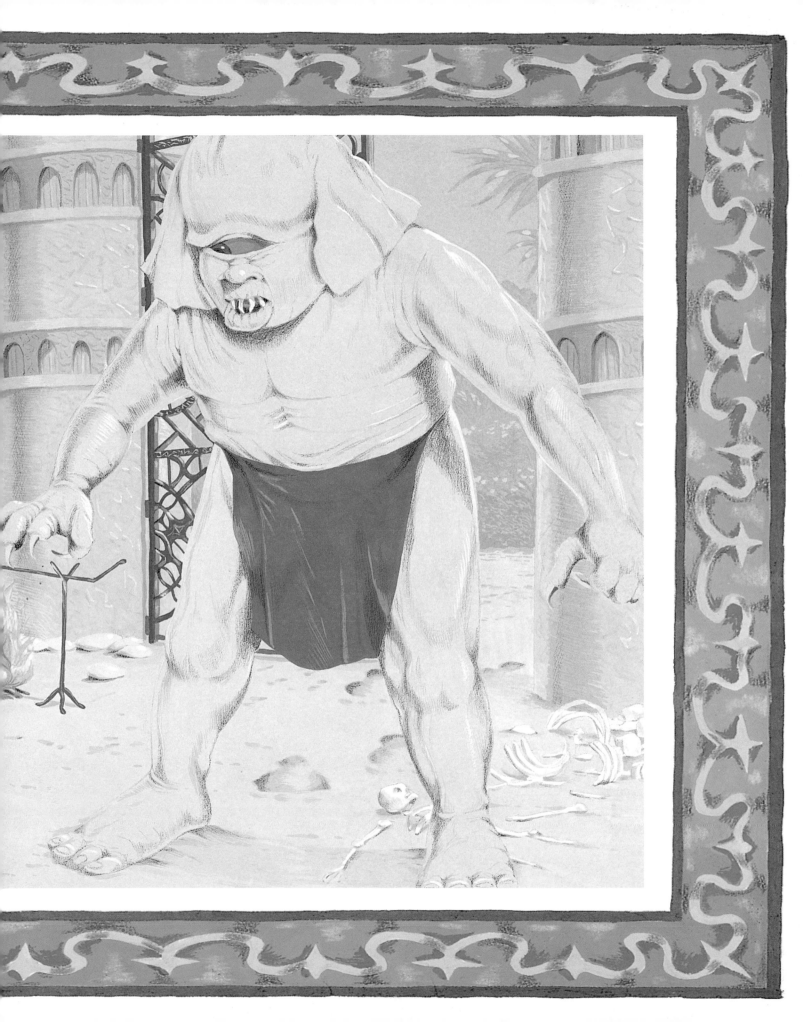

The beast plucked up one sailor and while the others watched in horror, roasted him on a spit and with much smacking of lips, ate him! Then the ogre fell asleep and his huge body blocked the gateway.

"We must try and kill him," whispered Sinbad. "If we take the red hot spits from the fire and push them in his eye he will surely die." So they crept up on the giant as he lay on his back and thrust the iron poles into his eye. The giant howled with pain and the sailors quickly made their escape. But the ogre was not dead and he chased them through the jungle and down to the beach. The terrified men leapt into the sea and swam for their lives while the ogre threw huge boulders after them. Many perished but lucky Sinbad survived with two other sailors.

At last the waves threw them upon another island and there another danger awaited them. A giant green lizard crept from the bushes and before they knew what was upon them, had gobbled down Sinbad's companions. Clever Sinbad lit a circle of fire around a tall tree then climbed into its branches. That night he was safe from the fearsome beast.

The next morning he saw a ship sail close by and, jumping from the tree he ran into the sea, shouting at the top of his voice. To his great relief, the Captain heard him and had soon pulled him on board.

After this Sinbad spent some time at home but after many months had passed he set sail once again. This time the ship ran out of food and the hungry sailors landed upon an unknown shore and set off in search of something to eat. To their delight they found a baby Roc hatching from its huge shell.

"Do not touch it!" cried Sinbad. "The mother Roc is a huge bird and will surely kill you," but the sailors paid him no heed and soon the infant Roc was roasting over a fire. Then the sky above them went dark and looking up, the sailors were horrified to see both mother and father Roc returning to their egg.

"To the ship! To the ship!" they cried as they ran pell mell down the beach. Soon the ship was fleeing the island, but the Rocs were in full pursuit. They bore huge rocks which they dropped upon the hapless sailors and soon the sea was full of drowning men. Good fortune was smiling again on Sinbad, for he was the only survivor.

At last the sea cast him upon an island and Sinbad set off to explore inland. He had not gone far when he came upon an old man sitting beside a brook.

"Please carry me across to the fruit trees on the other side," asked the old man pitifully. Sinbad gladly obliged but was shocked to find that the old man wrapped his legs around Sinbad's neck so strongly that he nearly passed out and at last fell down upon the ground. Then the old man gave him a mighty kick in the ribs and forced him up and onwards. All that day the old man ate fruit after fruit and at night he slept with his legs still locked tightly around Sinbad's head.

So it went on, day after day, and at last Sinbad thought of a plan. He squeezed a good amount of grape juice into an empty gourd and left it in the sun. After a while the juice turned into wine and Sinbad offered it to the old man.

"This is good," said the old man, swallowing it eagerly, and soon the gourd was empty. But the old man was drunk and danced so happily upon Sinbad's shoulders that he soon fell off! So at last Sinbad was free. Once again he hailed a passing ship and scrambled aboard.

After a time the ship landed at an island well known for its wonderful coconuts.

"This is how you gather them," a rich merchant told Sinbad. "Just copy me." Then he began throwing stones at the monkeys who clustered around the nuts at the top of the palm trees. The angry monkeys grabbed the nearest missiles to hand and soon coconuts were raining down upon the ground!

Sinbad traded his coconuts for spices and silks on his voyage around the islands but his next journey was to end once again in calamity. His ship was caught in a strong current which dragged it upon sharp rocks and the sailors were cast screaming overboard.

Sinbad found himself the sole survivor upon that rocky coast but there seemed to be no escape.

At last he found a small channel cut through the sheer rock face where the sea had forced a passage inland. He made himself a raft and, lashing himself to the timbers, set sail under the mountain. The current carried him through the dark for many hours but at last he emerged into bright sunshine and was found by a group of natives. They led him before their King and soon Sinbad was recounting his many exciting voyages to far off lands. The King was fascinated.

"Please return to your Sultan with gifts from the island of Serendib," he said, "but be sure to return soon for I would dearly love to hear more of your adventures."

So Sinbad arrived home with many costly presents which the Sultan was well pleased to receive.

"Now you must visit the King again," the Sultan told Sinbad. "We must repay his generosity with gifts of our own." So it was that Sinbad returned to the island of Serendib and was treated like a royal visitor.

At last he made his final farewells and set sail for home. He was getting old and wished to spend the rest of his days in the safe harbour of his house, surrounded by loving family and friends. The voyages of Sinbad the Sailor were over!